ARTEMIS

a tragedy of collage

MICHAEL BETANCOURT

Wildside Press

Wildside Press

www.wildsidepress.com

loneliness scherzo

on the way from here to there

we lose ourselves

Artemis looked back to see the silver thread stretched between the land and sky . . .

Artemis who had descended and returned sixty years later, no older . . .

Artemis who had traveled uncounted steps . . .

at the beginning . . .

Cycles present time without history:
the beginning is also the ending, which has gone before
and will come again.

PROLOGUE

stairway from heaven

0:1

thought palaces

       steal away before dawn comes

              cities now empty

forget the passions

       no longer is there dreaming

              just the ways home

standing guard over

       the body speaks its rage

              only loving lasts

no longer flesh

       the dream comes to power now

              and the day sleeps

nothing can stay long

       under the icy night

              lost songs fall deaf

colder sunlight

        fall upon the glass forest

                silenced birds sing

drift into twilight

        where distance appears

                near is far away

acid for the soul

        aqua regia of life

                leave nothing behind

truthful is painful

        bruised and beaten life goes on

                endings come too soon

through the long light

        darkness is waiting

                life remains there

0:3

ice spreads outward

  the lonely age has arrived

    all the dreamers flee

quiet thought cities

  scream without hearing the cry

    the songs are over

fleeting dreams

  nothing waits too long

    the night returns

an ending has come

  every start must someday stop

    and begin again

life requires death

  even the plants murder

    the circle is closed

flaming dream city

whose dark clouds glow and

hanging sparks fly

dreaming has stopped

smoke and flame shine bright

today dreams fail

ruin remains

a phoenix needs its ashes

fire is also birth

season pass away

gone in the dream times

nothing will wait

the future must kill

but always in the present

do the living die

0:5

the fallen shrine

        abandoned visions

                soon life will fade too

forever waiting

        a gateway to her past

                stretched too far now

feeling is fleeting

        everything falls into ruins

                monuments die

false hopes dream of truth

        into the future they pass

                bearing sole witness

a waiting guardian

        time passes slowly away

                but no one comes

daybreak is here

    anticipate the moment

        the night is leaving

time is the killer

    the past watches from the grave

        as the present dies

the night has passed

    quiet birds sing again

        now remembering

a silent song

    stretching across the sky

        lost memory

only the cycle

    daybreak and night falling

        leaves room for hope

the city poises

  at last time has come again

    tomorrow is here

steam vents shudder

  the sunlight has gone cold

    now winter draws near

forgetting her home

  the lonely way us shown too

    inside her dream

pronouncements

  made today are all the lies

    from a yesterday

chill winds blow down

  the streets stand empty still

    nothing grows here now

0:8

a dreaming city

    breathless air full of bird song

        the cold tortures

sparrows cry in pain

    crystal wind cuts them deeply

        no peace for them now

a hunter returns

    new victims await his grasp

        the cold burns like fire

winter came today

    remembering the ships sang

        a homeward dream . . .

to pause a moment
everyday will soon end
to start anew

each city rests
all fortunes wasting
dawn comes here too
through the seasons
winter, spring, summer, autumn
a cycle passes

formulations
an array of dark and light
fall across the mind

arrange the time
dreaming starlit nightfall
nothing waits now
silent birds
fly away from their roost
singing lost songs

remember it quick
a bright descending swallow
*blindness comes so fas*t

sunlight shining
on the way to the ending
only her hope
no more dreams
or abandoned bird song
leaving silence
now nightshade
night and day flow away
no more dreams here

memory fades
now is time to be resting
awaiting joy

LOGUE

her immobile journey

WINTER

The cold season of the year,
a period of gloom and sorrow,
the dark time.

She thought there was a problem
and tried to find it.

CHAPTER ONE

the sky in winter

1:1

the doors stand open

        as the moment draws neigh

                a cycle begun

the starlight dreams

        always follow the dark night

                the last mystery

the winter falls

        land sleeps a dark dream

                night strangles day

animal names

        the ancient mandate

                awaken to dream

the darkness spreads

        nightmares and passions

                know all the world

1:2

the MacNeal's Falcon

1:3

the Kleptor

1:4

the Ramdog

1:5

the Forynx

1:6

the Hexaped

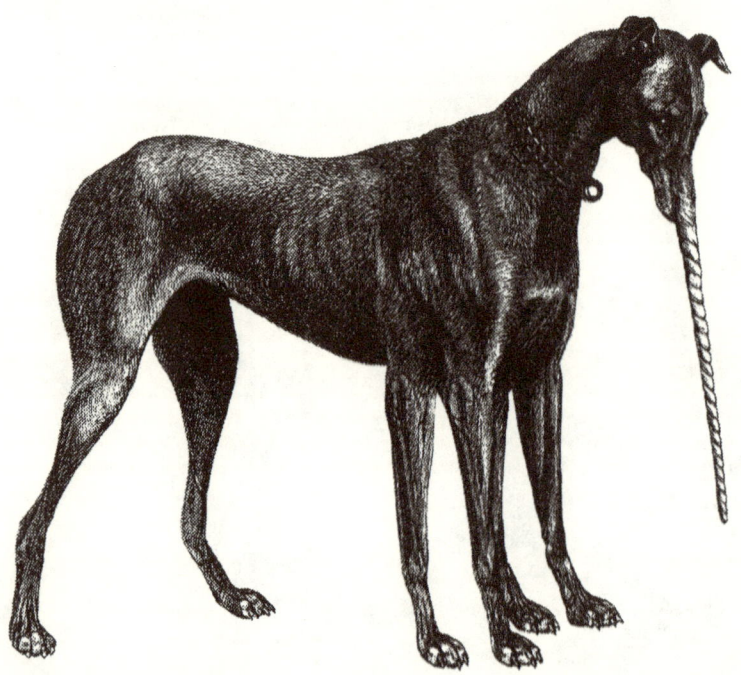

1:7

the Quacking Cow

1:8

the Horace,
  or Beakbird

SPRING

The season of the year when plants
begin to grow, to shoot up, or escape with
unexpected suddenness.

She didn't find the problem
and was disappointed

CHAPTER TWO

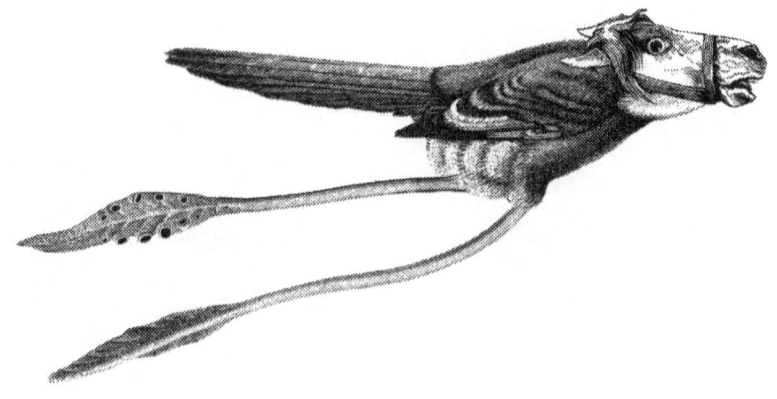

spring on the stairs

2:1

happily dancing

       along that cliff's edge

              once night flew

dominoes fall

       into the dream chasms

              nothing returns

starlight shows

       the path left untaken

              leaving the past

return her city

       off along the waterfall

              when day flees

look down from the sky

       now a height for laughing

              with forgotten joy

2:2

the Teonachto

2:3

the Hardoon

2:4

the Pfut

2:5

the Snowcat

2:6

the Herald's Swallow

2:7

the Koru-Kora

2:8

the Libbord

SUMMER

The warmest season of the year,
a happy and prosperous period
of light and growth.

She expected a problem and
was surprised by its absence.

CHAPTER THREE

the forest of summer

3:1

city of the dream

        when shall you fall to ruin

                shall the dream die too

stormy nightmares

        an icy fire burns too cold

                no solice found

journey homeward

        taking the long path

                colder nights pass

always dreaming

        nothing but the ruins

                remains today

once the dreams end

        wakeful birds go flying

                tomorrow calls

3:2

the Bleakwyrm

3:3

the Omatu

3:4

the Drunge,

or Quacking Ox

3:5

the Snortlebeast

3:6

the Groper

3:7

the Seafox

3:8

the Pestular Whale

AUTUMN

The season when the weather changes from
warm to cold, a period of decline and decay
when age and death arrive.

She thought she had found the problem,
but was mistaken.

CHAPTER FOUR

autumn by the ocean

4:1

a sleeping reason

    all her sins remembered

        the night comes quick

history forgets

    she saw magical places

        inside her dream

now anchor her here

    in the place where ships sang

        to remember now

know the way back home

    and the quiet waterfall

        her absent love

searching for a time

    to find herself a new sky

        her dream is over

4:2

the Arthur's Lizard

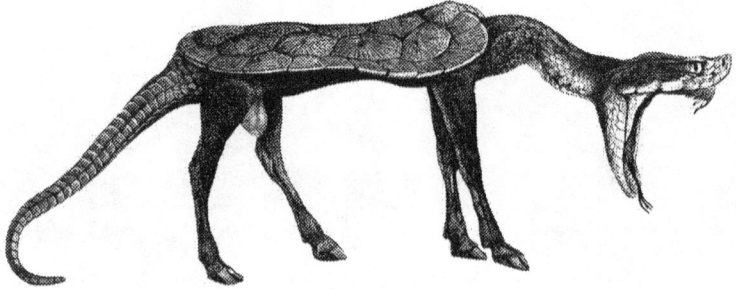

4:3

the Flying Jummie

4:4

the Equinnicks

4:5

the Parwhale

4:6

the Bobbie,

    or Hopping Rat

4:7

the Land Eel

4:8

remember times past

      where the distance we see

            is the ruin of dreams

city of the mind

      fall away from her dream now

            and lie crumbling

there is nothing left

      just a vision remains

            from what she once saw

. . . at the ending

By imagining there was a problem and searching for it,
she made it become real,
and her dreams became toxic.

EPILOGUE

people on the stairs

There were legends, of course.

But none remembered the builders of the great stairs: the stairs that climb and recede from the great sky ocean to the ball of the earth, the fiery orb of the sun sailing around them both. The steps themselves stretch beyond counting, each a single slab of stone set into a continuous spiral rising upwards until, at the summit, they open out onto a narrow harbor where the ships of the ocean people come to rest for trade and other things.

To the people who lived, laughed and loved on the edge of the waters, the stairs were simply there, standing at the base of their great city of sea grass and leather, a single fixed point at the center of their world. Only the priests knew the truth that the stairs continued downwards, without end in sight, vanishing into the gray, sourceless light of the deeper passage. Nothing that ever went down into that depth ever returned to their world. The mystery of the stairs was the holiest of holies, seen only by their highest priests, simply a phantom of myth to the rest of their people. Proof of the stairs was not needed toquestion their presence was to doubt the very basis of their world. The stairs stood at the pivot of the world.

The stairs were their way to the afterlife, the proof that the gods had created their city and them as the chosen people of their world. It was the unquestionable fact of the stairs' presence that protected the city, sprawling across the smooth surface of the ocean, edgeless, wall-less, stretching from horizon to horizon on pontoons and ancient ships built from strange materials unseen on the waters. The traders who visited the City of the Stairs could only stare in wonder at the streets of smooth water and the boatmen who carried passengers from one quarter to another. It was a city built on legend.

It was known all across the waters, a city grown fat on its unknown past.

In the ages since the building of the stairwell, the people at the top had forgotten that the stairs led somewhere, a fact only the theologians would mention quietly and in private, for to suggest that the stairs were not a physical proof of the existence of the gods was heresy. And yet, the stairs were there. And occasionally one of the theologians would simply disappear, drawn to the mystery of the stairs and the unknown that they suggested.

The stairs themselves were nothing special. Simply a circular well a hundred feet across, they started at the top and simply spiraled down within the cylinder, but not into darkness, simply into a gray half-light that came from nowhere and everywhere and would make walking them dangerous since the walls and the steps were also gray. It was simply a descent into evenness, where distances and spaces simply dissolved into one another, and always the steps leading down, down. Stairs seeming without end.

The high priests, it was said, knew the truth about the stairs and their purpose, but kept that to themselves. The Gods never did something without reason, and it was the fear about what that reason might be that kept the city safe; no invading navy ever attempted to conquer it.

Nothing that happened in the city was so slight, so minor as to be accounted for within their encyclopedic ceremonies. Every possibility a page in their holy books, every change a heresy. Religious tradition served in place of history. The will of the Gods was the teachings of the priests and that will was absolute. Time stood poised, unpassing on the waters as the city hung between its reflection and the sky, sustained by priests whose rites orchestrated each moment of each day and night with music, smoke and dance prescribed by sacred decree.

The city's residents knew with the absolute certainty of those who have been told a lie so many times that it has become truth, for such was the false knowledge encouraged by the priests, that the stairs were a myth: no more than a story set down as metaphor for their afterlife journey, provenin stone, areward from which no one returns. To allow belief otherwise was to encourage the curious. The people of the city were not allowed to know the reality of the stairs; the priests allowed the belief that no one living could descend and return.

So while the citizens of the city believed that none had ever returned from traveling on the stairs, the high priests knew the legend of Artemis. Artemis the theologian. Artemis the legend. Artemis the heretic. Artemis who returned.

Artemis who descended the stairs and impossibly returned sixty years later, no older than when she left. Artemis who had walked the uncounted steps to the base of the stairwell, where the last step touches the ground and the only way to continue is to turn back. The long climb towards the city in the sky an ascent towards heaven. To stand at the base and gaze out and up into the sky, a silver thread joining the earth to the heavens, was to realize that the stairs were more than simply a well. They were tying heaven and earth, a silver line with the world of sky and land pulled taught at either end.

The final step, the wall with a doorway, the opening to a plain of golden sand rolling away. Artemis told her story about the world at the base of the stairs, beyond the final step, a place where the deck was not a deck, and the air was dry. Trees rose from the ground, their branches stretching into finer and finer hairs to catch the sun's rays with their lapis leaves. Nothing on the waters at the top of the stairs could compare with the chimes those leaves made in the gentle breeze, or the songs of the night birds chasing one another through those leaves, golden eyes ever watchful for the snakes that twined themselves around the great trunks of the trees, their nets of golden wire always in wait.

The story Artemis told was a lie.

There were no trees of lapis, night birds or snakes with nets of fine gold. The desert she saw was not really a desert at all, but a forest of dunes and small villages whose people accepted her as their guest. It was on the long climb downwards that she grew into her fantasy of a land at the end waiting for her, with magical creatures and impossible plants. She grew so lonely on her long walk that she failed to see the many people who lived on the stairs themselves, tending to their flocks grazing on the grasses that grew from the cracks between the stairs, eking out a simple existence, drinking from the wall fountains every few miles, their streams of crystal water flowing down, over the stairs, to pool at landings miles below.

The distances she traveled gradually stretched towards the infinite in their monotony, stretching her sense of time until it stopped passing. Always the stairs remained before her feet, unchanging, making it impossible to tell how far she had come or still had to go. Each step always appeared the same as the previous.

The stairs stretched onwards, ever on, before, behind. No different, no farther from home, no closer to her destination, no changes for her eyes to see as she walked. The nothing of the stairs extending to infinity.

Knowing about the beginnings and endings Artemis saw behind her shiny eyes, the herders let her pass, her eyes glassy with the fantasy life she led down among the people at the foot of the stairs, her nights filled with dreams of a city of rafts and derelict ships clustered around the summit of the great stair. She was a ghost to them: the herders and their wives simply watched her pass, doing nothing but keep their children safe. She had the wandering sickness, the disease that strikes only the very ancient and sends them away into their fantasies of the beginning and end. For the herders there were only the steps and the fountains and their flocks. For them there was no religion, simply the ever present need to move on, to find the fresh pastures that always lie beyond the next step.

Wandering sickness simply happened to the ancient ones, the ones who had lived too long and begun to wonder too much about the stairs themselves rather than taking the world as it was, with no place for change, their childhood doubts and questions returning to assail them. All points were the same. And so Artemis passed through the herders and they passed around her, each failing to acknowledge the other. To Artemis, the herders were simply phantoms of her loneliness and isolation on the stairs.

Each night she would dream her arrival-return to the city on the water and the forest along the dunes, calling the names of the animals that dwelt there: the Koru-Kora, the Hardoon, the Pestular Whale, the Omatu and all the other animals of the mind. Ferocious, she would name each and send it on its way back into the twinkling of the night.

The journey down and back took forever for Artemis, even though little time passed on her long walk, each day beginning simply when she woke and ending only when exhaustion consumed her so much that she had to lie on the steps and sleep. Neither day nor night but the unending twilight of her march into the depths. So long that she lost track of her steps, the count becoming countless.

And Artemis returned to the entrance where she had descended an eternity before to find her fantasy of the city she thought she dreamed remained, but her memory of what she had seen and done in the journey down the stairs had grown gray as the eternal twilight of the stairs. In the time she spent climbing the stairs, passing through the herders and their small flocks, their children playing like ghosts, she had lost herself, herself become a ghost among ghosts.

And so Artemis told her stories about the snakes and the birds and the trees with their lapis leaves and songs she heard at night echoing through the far reaches of the tunnel as she descended never realizing that it was her voice singing the songs, inventing the words, calling out the melodies. In passing through the ghostly herders she didn't hear their voices saying she had the wandering sickness, that she dreamed her way in the world.

She was never sure if she actually saw the herders or simply imagined them in her loneliness, in the monotony of the stairs continuing forever.

So much time had passed for Artemis that when she emerged, she no longer believed in her city shehad dreamed her return so many nights thinkingthat she was still asleep on the stairs, simply awaiting the moment to awaken and see the steps stretch before her, uncertain if she had arrived, would ever arrive.

towards fallen hope

      how many miles remain

            homewards and homewards

within our dreams

      all the hearts desires

            granted with a cost

harsh light of night

      nothing shines so clearly

            as her faded desire

looking backward

      where shall the city go now

            nothing ever lasts

even stories end

      and the dreaming stops again

            a final ending

. . . in the cycle . . .

The tragedy lies in the cycle of history:
that which has gone before will come again;
this, too, is the hope.

. . . a lost dream
journey without ending
the path goes on . . .

ABOUT THE AUTHOR

Artemis is Michael Betancourt's second collage novel. While he makes visual art and has exhibited it internationally, he is better known as a theorist and movie maker.